Josephine Wants to Dance

by Jackie French illustrated by Bruce Whatley

Abrams Books for Young Readers
New York

Library of Congress Cataloging-in-Publication Data:
French, Jackie.
  Josephine wants to dance / by Jackie French ; illustrated by Bruce Whatley.
      p. cm.
  Summary: Despite the discouragement of her little brother, Joey, Josephine proves that kangaroos can, indeed,
become dancers when she fills in for an injured prima ballerina.
  ISBN-13: 978-0-8109-9431-7 (hardcover)
  ISBN-10: 0-8109-9431-3 (hardcover)
  [1. Dance—Fiction. 2. Ballet dancing—Fiction. 3. Kangaroos—Fiction. 4. Brothers and sisters—Fiction. 5.
Australia—Fiction.] I. Whatley, Bruce, ill. II. Title.
  PZ7.F88903Jos 2007
  [E]—dc22
                                        2006100213

Text copyright © Jackie French 2006
Illustrations copyright © Farmhouse Illustration Company Pty Limited 2006
The Author and the Illustrator have asserted their right to be identified as the Author and the Illustrator of this work.

Book design by Vivian Cheng

First published in English in Sydney, Australia by HarperCollins Publishers Australia Pty Ltd. in 2006.
This American edition is published by arrangement with HarperCollins Publishers Australia Pty Ltd.

Printed and bound in China
10 9 8 7 6 5 4 3 2 1

HNA ▮▮▮▮▮
harry n. abrams, inc.
a subsidiary of La Martinière Groupe

115 West 18th Street
New York, NY 10011
www.hnabooks.com

To Fuchsia, the roo who danced around our lives,
and to Bruce, who turns words into magic.
—J. F.

To my new friend Phoebe R, who loves to line dance.
—B. W.

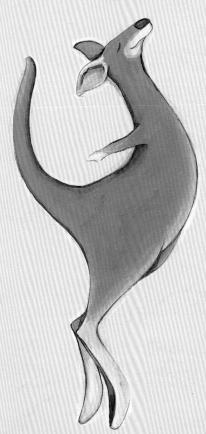

Josephine loved to dance.

Josephine lived in Australia, where

she bounced with the brolgas . . .

and leaped with the lyrebirds.

"Kangaroos don't dance,
Josephine!"
said her little brother, Joey.
"They hop."

But Josephine took no notice.

The emus showed her how to point her toes.
The eagles taught her how to soar
to the music of the wind.

Josephine whirled like the clouds above the river.
She swayed like the branches in the trees.

But still she dreamed of somehow finding another way to dance.

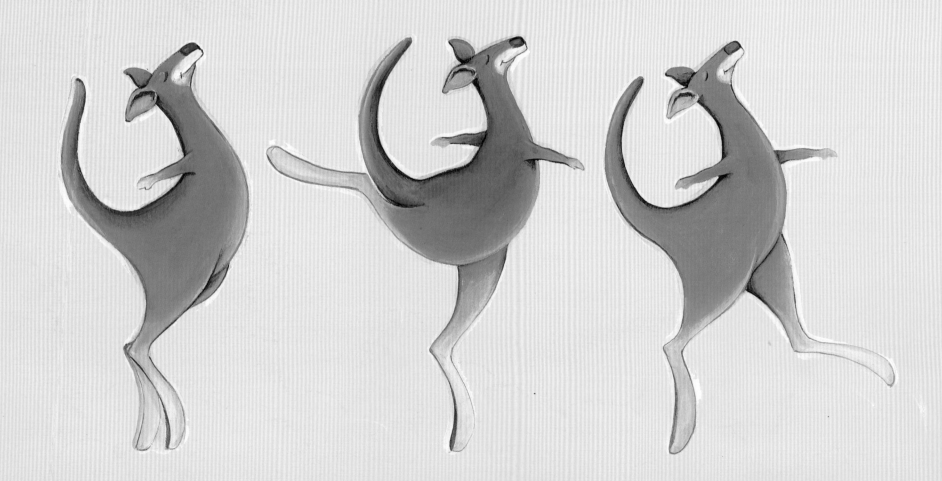

"There has to be something **more!**"
said Josephine wistfully as she danced
over her brother.

"**Kangaroos don't
dance, Josephine!**"
yelled Joey, ducking his head.

"**They jump.**"

But Josephine kept
on dancing.

The next day Josephine found posters stuck on the trees. The ballet was coming to the town of Shaggy Gully!

"**That's** how I'd like to dance!" cried Josephine. "In a pink tutu, with silk ballet shoes."

"Get real!" said Joey. "Kangaroos don't wear tutus, Josephine! And they **never** wear silk ballet shoes."

"**I'm** going to," said Josephine, pointing her toes.

She crept over to the hall . . .

and peered through the window as the dancers rehearsed.

A week later Josephine sneaked into town.

"Ohhh!" cried Josephine.

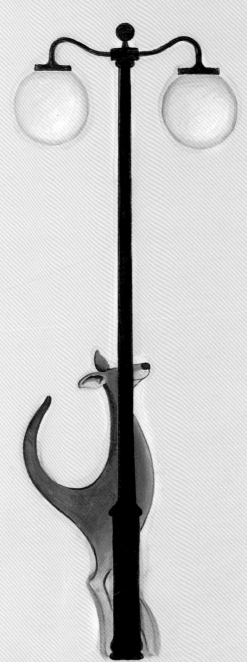

She watched the dancers for hours.
Then she practiced at night . . . all alone.

She spun, she swirled, she pirouetted . . .
and at the end she always curtsied.

"I really **am** becoming a dancer now,"
thought Josephine.

The day of the first
performance arrived.
But the ballet company
was in trouble!

"Ow!" shrieked the prima ballerina as she twisted her ankle.
"Ohhh!" sobbed the understudy as she found a splinter in her toe.

"Who will dance the lead role?"

cried the ballet director.

"Who else can leap so high?"

Josephine jumped . . .

through the window . . .
    and onto the stage.

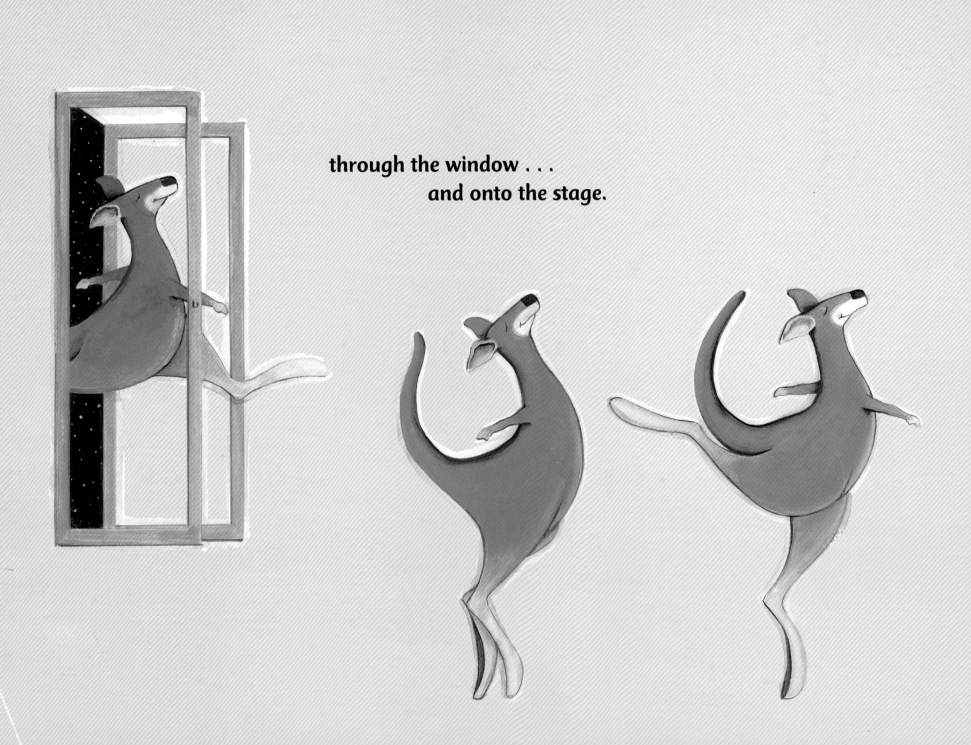

"A kangaroo!" yelled the dancers.

"There's a kangaroo on the stage!"

Josephine pointed her toes. She tossed her head.
She swayed like the lyrebirds as they call to their sweethearts.
She soared like an eagle through the sky.

"A **dancing** kangaroo!" everyone cried.

"Who ever heard of a dancing kangaroo?"

Josephine swirled above the stage like the mist playing with the moon.

The director stared at Josephine.
Finally, she smiled. "Well, this kangaroo
can dance—and she knows the lead role.
And she can jump higher than
any other dancer I've seen!"

The director took Josephine
to the wardrobe department.

"A kangaroo!" exclaimed the costume designer.
"I can't dress a kangaroo!"

"Just do your best,"
the director told him.

The costume designer quickly
altered a tutu for Josephine.

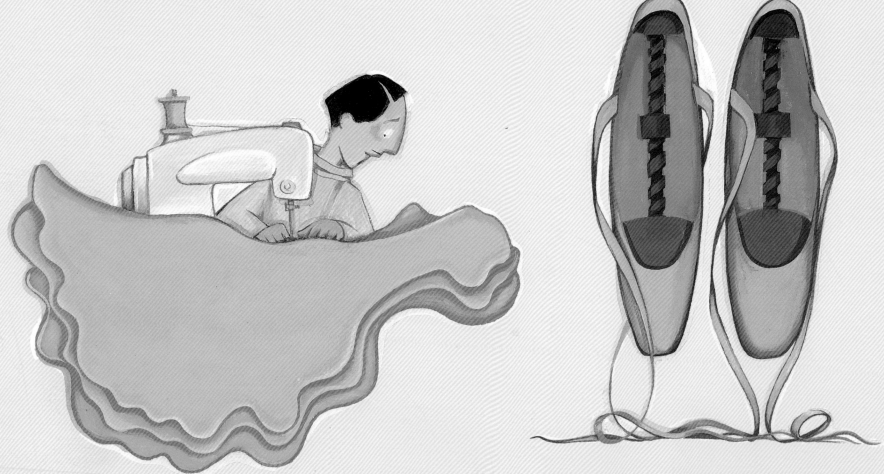

He stretched some ballet shoes, too.
They were probably the longest
ballet shoes in the world.

At last it was time
for the performance.
The audience took their seats.
The orchestra tuned up.

Josephine stood backstage,
waiting for the music to begin.

"Josephine!" hissed Joey
through the window.
"What are you doing?
Come back to the bush
at once!"

"No!" said Josephine.
"I'm going to dance. In a pink
tutu, with silk ballet shoes.
I'm going to jump higher than any
other dancer in the world!"

The lights dimmed.
The orchestra started playing.
The curtains opened.
The performance began.

The ballerinas fluttered onto the stage . . .   one . . .   two . . .   three . . .

four . . .   and . . .   **Josephine!**

Someone in the audience giggled. "It's a kangaroo!"

Then Josephine began to dance.

She twirled through the air like leaves in a whirlwind.

She leaped like no dancer ever had before.

And at the end she curtsied like the brolgas bowing to the sun.

The audience was silent.

And then they clapped.

And then they . . . cheered!

"**This kangaroo is a dancer!**" they cried.

"A truly **magnificent** dancer!"

Josephine was still curtsying
when the ballet director brought
bunches of roses onto the stage.

"Roses are delicious!" exclaimed Josephine.
"And I am finally a dancer—and it's **fun!**"

In fact, dancing
looked like so much
fun that soon all
the audience . . .

and leaping and thumping . . .

swishing and swirling . . .

and twinkle-toe twirling . . .

but nobody **ever** danced quite like . . .

Josephine!